Rowing To the Rescue

The Story of Ida Lewis,
Famous Lighthouse Heroine

by Doris Licameli

Pictures and illustrations are reproduced from the following sources:
Harper's Weekly, 1869; Frank Leslie's Illustrated Newspaper 1867,
1881; Scribner's Monthly, 1881; The Ladies Home Companion,
1890; The Ladies Home Journal, 1890; Newport Historical Society;
C. W. Nichols print by D. Appleton & Co., New York; stereoviews by
J. A. Williams and American Scenery; Old postcard pictures by H. C.
Leighton Co., Portland, Maine; The Rhode Island News Co.,
Providence, Rhode Island; Morris Berman, New Haven, Connecticut.
The USCGC Ida Lewis Insignia, courtesy of the United States Coast
Guard.

Cover Design by Emily Thompson, Thompson Studio

ISBN 978-1-84728-668-0

ACKNOWLEDGMENTS

Heartfelt thanks to Dolly and Mel Cebulash for their priceless wisdom and guidance. And to Robert Pouch, Executive Director of the State of New York Board of Commercial Pilots, and Bertram Lippincott III, Reference Librarian at the Newport Historical Society, for so generously giving their time to read my manuscript and offer helpful comments. I'm also indebted to the great folks at the Fairview Public Library, who've always helped me every which way and then some; and to Brian Stinson, who kindly shared his wealth of knowledge regarding Ida Lewis.

But most of all, my eternal gratitude goes to my loving family for nourishing me with their Faith and Cheers.

Sometimes the spray dashes against these windows so thick I can't see out, and for days at a time the waves are so high that no boat would dare come near the rock, not even if we were starving. But I am happy....

Ida Lewis

Contents

Leaving Spring Street

The old wooden door creaked and clanked shut.
Echoes traveled through the morning stillness, up into
the velvety blue Rhode Island sky.

Ida clutched her dog Matey tighter to her chest,
fighting off a strange feeling of gloom. It was the last time
she'd be hearing those familiar sounds. Today was
moving day.

The government had finally built Father a *real*
lighthouse to tend out on the lime rocks, a live-in kind
for the whole family. He'd no longer be rowing across
Newport harbor day and night in every kind of weather to
light and refuel what had been nothing but a mere
lantern hanging in a little tower out there.

But it meant leaving Spring Street behind!

"Let's be on our way," Mother said, tucking the key into her pocket. "Father's been waiting at the wharf long enough." Her long gray skirt swirled around her ankles as she strode away, toting the family Bible in both arms.

Ida knew that the first page of the sacred book, where important Lewis family events were always listed, already held today's special entry: *Moving Day, June 25, 1857.*

Thomas Rudolph, better known as Rud, whooped with joy and darted away. Hosea Jr. and little Hattie scrambled after him, sending their own happy cries into the air.

Ida, eldest of the four children, watched them go. But she didn't move. She *couldn't* move. Her feet felt anchored to the spot.

She wrinkled her brow as she threw another glance up and down Spring Street. *How deeply will I miss this place?* she wondered with a heaviness in her heart. In all her fifteen years she'd always lived among these familiar shops and houses, where everything was so blessedly close at hand. Especially her best friend, Mary.

"Idawalley Zoradia Lewis, must we pry you from the spot?" Mother called over her shoulder.

With a deep sigh, Ida set her gloomy thoughts free. Then she hurried toward her family, reminding herself how joyful she'd been when Father first brought home his good news.

Besides, she'd forgotten that come September she'd be back in town almost *every day*. Hattie and the boys, too. Only now they'd have to cross the harbor's waters to get to school!

The Lime Rock Light

The lighthouse rowboat rocked lazily near the wharf. After ferrying household furnishings across the harbor since dawn, it seemed to be waiting patiently for the day's last trip.

"Ahoy, Father!" Ida called as she marched down the sandy slope toward the water.

She loved the way her father always returned a greeting with a gentle tipping of his faded, peaked cap. The hat was a remnant from his days as a coast pilot. In sun, wind or rain, he'd leave his own boat and climb the rope ladder that hung down the side of a waiting ship. Once aboard he'd bring the vessel safely through the harbor to a docking place, steering clear of the shoals, hidden rocks and sunken ships that lurked dangerously below. To this day people still called him *Captain* Lewis.

Without being asked, Ida helped settle everyone into the swaying rowboat before stepping gingerly aboard herself. Then she wound the mooring rope into a coil and set it at her feet near Matey's curly black tail before drawing Hattie onto her lap.

"Hold tight!" Father cried, pushing away from the wharf. As he pulled hard on the oars in steady rhythm, a tiny smile peeked out from the center of his wavy gray whiskers. It was all Ida needed to rid herself of any lingering sadness over leaving Spring Street. She smiled back at him, and it truly felt good.

Sunbeams danced all across the water like glittering diamonds, parting in a path as the boat creaked and moaned its way through. Ida watched for a while, nearly hypnotized. Then she turned her gaze straight ahead, toward the new Lime Rock Light.

The square white building was two stories high, with a gently pointing roof. Gazing at it now, Ida remembered someone calling it Classical Greek Revival style. That prompted a funny notion. *Imagine that! The Lewis family of Newport, Rhode Island, with a little Greek palace and an island all their own.*

When Ida repeated the thought aloud, no one laughed harder than Father.

Soon enough, they reached the rocky shore.

Hattie and the boys raced toward the house, laughing at the sight of Matey galloping along in their wet tracks. Mother trailed them at a slower pace across the slippery rocks.

But Ida stayed behind. She would help Father carry the last of the moving-day packages up to the house, though not before he tied up the boat good and tight. Perish the thought it might drift itself back to Newport, stranding them with no way off the island except on the back of an oversized seagull!

As she waited, Ida looked out over the harbor, enjoying the sight of puffy white sails gliding back and forth. A steady breeze, smelling of salt, whipped her skirt and tousled her hair into loose, messy wisps. She took in deep breaths and listened contentedly to the soothing whisper of the waves as they washed in and out.

"This seems such a peaceful place," she said.

Father looked up. He took his chewed-up pipe from his mouth and nodded slightly. "Aye, but you must keep in mind it won't always be so."

Drawing closer, he set his hands gently on Ida's shoulders. His eyes seemed to cloud over. "When a fierce tempest is blowing with howling winds and battering sea, this pile of rocks can be a rightly godawful place. You must be prepared for *that*, too."

Ida felt her stomach tighten. She knew Father hadn't meant to scare her. It was just his truthful way. Still, the grim warning hung darkly in her mind as they walked toward the house together.

Surprise At The Lighthouse

Once Ida stepped through the open doorway, all was forgotten. The house was finer than she'd ever imagined, with cheery whitewashed walls, new wood-planked floors, and nice tall windows that let in plenty of sunshine.

Standing there admiring it all, Ida suddenly remembered recent hints of a surprise that might be waiting for her in the bedroom she'd be sharing with Hattie. Her short leather boots tapped over the floor as she darted toward the stairs.

"Not so fast," Mother said, looking up. She'd taken the lid off the packing barrel near the kitchen table, ready to start digging out the contents. "There's work to be done."

Ida shrugged in compliance and tied on an apron. Determined to get the chore done fast, she practically whirled around the kitchen setting pots, crocks, and dishes on shelves and wall hooks, wherever Mother directed.

Thankfully, there was less settling-in work to be done in the parlor and sitting room. All they needed were Mother's treasured lace curtains at the windows.

Ida handled the delicate white panels with careful fingers. She knew they were something of a luxury. Mother said they'd been handed down from her own parents, along with the silver candleholders and matching snuffer sitting next to the Bible on the tea table. Grandfather Willey had been a doctor over on Block Island and well able to afford such fine things, though Ida knew her mother cherished them more for sentimental value than their cost.

As soon as the curtains were fluttering like angel wings across the open windows, Ida threw off her apron and rushed upstairs, two steps at a time.

When she poked her head through the bedroom doorway, her eyes widened with delight. Her very own bed! No more enduring Hattie's restless little arms and legs through the night. She had no doubt Hattie, small as she was, would be happy, too, having their narrow old bed all to *her* self.

Stepping closer, Ida stared hard at the bed's unusual headboard. It was painted with a colorful scene. A *sinking ship!*

She couldn't help thinking a bouquet of pretty flowers might've been more helpful for a good night's sleep. But after her first impression subsided, she broke out in a wry grin.

"I suppose *this* is more fitting for a lighthouse," she said to herself.

Then her eyes traveled to the blank wall above her bed. Here was the perfect spot for the hand-painted print Mary gave her for her birthday that past February, a gift Mother had openly considered very strange.

Grace Darling

Drawn by the *thump, thump, thump* against the wall,
Hattie poked her curly head through the doorway. She
looked up at the new addition on the wall and wrinkled
her nose.

"Why do you want a picture of a *grave* over your bed,
Ida?"

Ida sighed. "To begin with, the tomb of Grace Darling is
a famous place. It pays tribute to a brave English

heroine, someone I deeply admire. She lived in a lighthouse, just as we do now."

Ida sat at the edge of the bed and drew Hattie onto her lap to continue her favorite story. "One day in 1838 Grace awoke to a wretched storm. When she looked through her telescope she spied people clinging to a shipwreck. She begged her father to help, over and over, until he finally agreed."

A frown puckered Hattie's face. "How could they help those people from inside the lighthouse?"

Ida shook her head. "Not from inside," she said quickly. "Grace and her father rowed a mile through fierce wind and churning sea to reach the wreck. Then, with strength and courage people don't usually expect of a young woman, Grace managed to keep the boat steady while her father took five drowning seamen into the boat. After rowing back to the lighthouse, Grace tended to the men while her father went back and saved four more lives."

Pure admiration glowed in Ida's gray eyes. But Hattie only frowned harder. "I'd be too scared to row a boat into a storm."

"Hattie, those poor souls would've *died* if not for Grace!"

Almost instantly, Ida regretted her foolish vexation. She drew in a deep breath then took her little sister's hand and squeezed it gently, lovingly.

"I think we should go outside and see what wonderful adventure Rud and Hosea are up to."

The Beacon

The evening sky melted from vivid blue to a spectacular explosion of orange, pink and purple. Ida thought it the finest sunset she'd ever seen. She could have gazed through the kitchen window forever, but the last of the dinner dishes were waiting to be dried.

"Time to light the beacon," Father said, walking into the kitchen. He took a candle down from the shelf. "Care to come up and watch me work?"

Ida nearly burst with delight. Of course she would! She'd always appreciated that *her* father involved her in teachings most others only shared with *sons*. How else could she have learned such interesting things as tying intricate sailors' knots and foretelling changes in the weather by studying the birds and clouds?

The lantern room was a small, square extension built on the side of the house. Ida followed her father through the dark, narrow passageway across the hall from her bedroom, glancing at the eerie wall shadows that moved along with them in the candlelight.

"Oh, my!" she gasped when she saw the new light. It looked like an amazing glass *behive.*

"It's a sixth-order Fresnel lens," Father said. He explained how the unique arrangement of lenses and prisms would turn the glow from an inner oil lamp into a far-reaching beam.

"I'm told by many a grateful ship's captain these new Fresnels are far better aids to navigation than anything used before. So I reckon they're worth every minute of the special care they need."

Ida smiled knowingly. Eager to learn more, she watched intently as Father grabbed his supplies one by one. Brass oilcans, measuring cups, wicks and just about everything else he needed were sitting on a nearby wall shelf, beneath a tacked-up Lighthouse Board document titled *Instructions to Keepers.*

The lamp got a good wiping with a special cloth before Father filled the well with oil. "Even the smallest bit of residue could have a bad effect," he said.

Then he selected a wick from the tin and began snipping this way and that.

"Wrong size?" Ida asked, suddenly puzzled.

Father shook his head as he snipped. "The tip has to be exactly even for the brightest, safest flame."

He nodded toward the tacked-up instructions and said the Board suggests doing this every four hours through the night. "Might be why some keepers call themselves *wickies.*"

Ida thought about this a few seconds. All things considered, she supposed spending so much time tending to the wick of a lamp was as good a reason as any for the funny title.

Soon enough, the beacon was aglow.

Ida hurried to the window. Her smile deepened when she saw the bright trail cutting through the darkened waters below like a shining path to safety.

Then Father appeared at her side. "Always remember that no matter what happens, this light *must* burn every night." His tone was suddenly somber. "Sailors depend on it for their very *lives.*"

The memory of the vivid painting on her headboard flashed brightly in Ida's head. Though the evening was still warm, she felt as if a gust of winter air had swept over her. But she managed a slight nod to let her father know she truly understood.

Sudden Change

As summer wore on Ida enjoyed her new home more each day, especially having the unpredictable sea at her doorstep. In no time at all she taught herself to swim the salty swells with such perfection Father jokingly warned that people might mistake her for a new kind of fish and try to reel her in.

Then Ida turned her sights on the lighthouse rowboat. She was determined to master the oars, though she soon discovered it was far from an easy task. She was small and slim, weighing hardly more than a handful of fog, according to the other girls in her class. And the boat was big and clumsy. There were times it even seemed to have a mind of its own!

But as Father liked to say, once a thought anchored in Ida's mind, there was no stopping her.

By late August Ida was racing about the busy harbor as if the rowboat had wings. For a long while her joyful grin was met only by gaping, curious stares. There were even times when she'd seen grizzled old sailors drop jaw and pipe as she flew by. But she could only wonder why.

Then one day in Mr. Allen's general store over on Thames Street, Ida heard two fancy-dressed ladies whispering as she passed by. "It's that lighthouse girl," one voice hissed.

Ida was stunned. They were talking about her! She stole a quick glance their way. Their crisp white linen dresses and big, plumed hats told her they were well-to-do summer visitors, probably up from New York or Philadelphia. More than likely they lived in one of those huge mansions popping up all over Newport.

"I'm told by some who've seen with their own eyes that she not only *swims;* but she's probably the fastest swimmer in all of Newport!" the hissy voice continued. "They say she rows a boat better than any man, too, if you can believe *that.*"

"Hmmph!" said the other voice haughtily. "Certainly not activities for a *proper* young lady."

So that's it! Ida thought. She buried her nose deeper in her shopping list, struggling to keep her mischievous grin from their prying eyes. *Well, if you ask me,* proper *young ladies are missing out on a lot of great fun!*

28

Ida thought the fun would last forever.

Then one Sunday in October, barely four months after moving to the Lime Rock Light, Ida heard words that took her breath away.

"Your father's had a stroke," Dr. King said gravely as he tiptoed from the bedroom alongside Mother. "He's paralyzed."

No! Not Father! Ida wanted to cry out. Tears threatened at the corners of her eyes. But she blinked them back to where they came from. She told herself crying wouldn't help things one bit. She had to stay strong.

After rowing Dr. King back to Newport, Ida huddled on the rocks with her frightened little sister and brothers, all of them staring aimlessly toward the horizon. Matey seemed to sense their broken hearts and curled close at their feet.

"What will happen to us?" asked Rud, sniffling back tears. His rowdy, ten-year-old-boy antics were gone, as if blown out to sea in a storm.

Hosea, taking a cue from his big brother, began to whimper, too. "Will we have to leave the lighthouse?"

Ida was still trembling deep inside. But she forced a confident tone. "Of course not. Mother said it's not at all unusual for wives to take over lighthouse duties if something happens to their husbands."

In truth, Ida knew her mother couldn't do everything alone. It was up to her to lend a hand.

Though she'd always loved school, Ida never returned. Her days were too full of work, helping Mother with household chores, Father's nursing care, and tending the beacon.

Besides all that, she had to row back and forth across the harbor every day to fetch supplies and get the young ones to the schoolhouse in town.

Ida seldom thought about Spring Street anymore. But when she did, it seemed a very long time ago.

Then to Ida's disbelief, tragedy struck again just a short time later. Now Hattie fell gravely ill. Dr. King called it consumption, a dreaded disease that ravaged people's lungs.

Ida thought her heart would break into pieces when she looked at her sweet little sister lying limply in bed, as ashen as the sheets all around her. Only five years old and so close to death!

But Ida buried her sorrow deep inside again. It was up to her to carry on now that Mother had little time for anything but nursing *two* sick people.

Teenage Lighthouse Keeper

Every day at sunset, Ida climbed the steps to the lantern room. She wiped the lamp spotless, filled the well with oil, and trimmed the wick to perfection. At midnight, she returned to do it all again.

"Don't worry," she'd tell Father with a teasing smile, hoping to soothe the constant worry in his watery eyes. "I promise you, the light shines just as brightly as if *you* were the one snipping at the wick."

But sometimes she stared sleeplessly from her bed for hours, especially during stormy weather. She had to be sure the beacon still glowed. Sailors depended on her for their lives and she couldn't let them down!

With each dawn came a new day's work. After donning a special linen apron that wouldn't scratch the delicate lenses, Ida extinguished the light. Then she measured the amount of oil consumed during the night and entered it in the keeper's journal. Weather conditions were set down, too.

Just as Father had instructed that first night at the lighthouse, she cleaned every trace of soot and oil from the inner lamp then polished lenses and brass frame until they gleamed back her thin face. After that, she swept the lantern room floor and passageway steps carefully with a damp hand brush so no flying sooty specks landed back on the lantern.

Ida always made sure to be finished by ten o'clock each morning. The Lighthouse Board demanded it, and she never dared disobey. Though the schedule required the District Inspector to sail up from New York every three months, he sometimes made surprise visits. And that could mean trouble if he discovered something he didn't like.

Ida had seen with her own eyes the scrutinizing way the inspector walked through the house with his clipboard, checking to see if everything was clean and orderly. He even peeked under beds!

It was a well-known fact that keepers not following the Board's strict instructions could be put out of work, so Ida was exceedingly careful. She dreaded to think what might become of her family if she were to get bad marks.

In between chores, rowing back and forth to town was still part of Ida's day, no matter the weather. There were times when she'd traveled home in icy water up to her knees after angry waves had splashed into the boat. Her frozen stockings had to be cut away from her thin legs when she got home.

"I wish life was kinder to you," Mother said one such wintry evening as she tried to drive the blue from Ida's legs with a wrap of warm towels.

Ida pretended not to see the tears in her mother's weary eyes. "Pay it no mind," she said with a cheery shrug. "I *like* doing a man's job." It was a truth that came straight from her heart. Unlike dreary housework, her keeper's duties seemed to fill her with a sense of freedom.

The last time Ida saw Mary in town she'd confessed the very same thing to her dear friend. Mary had laughed knowingly when Ida added that she actually *enjoyed* fighting the waves.

"Smooth waters aren't any fun. I much prefer a good battle with rough seas!"

A Heroine Is Born

One drab afternoon the following autumn Ida paused at the kitchen window to steal a moment's rest. The low sky loomed as gray as the pewter pitcher on the nearby shelf. Frothy whitecaps churned across the harbor waters. There was no doubt in Ida's mind. Another gale was ready to blow.

She was about to turn away when something on the water caught her eye. Four boys were frolicking dangerously in a sailboat, halfway between the lime rocks and Fort Adams to the west.

Ida stared in disbelief when one boy actually climbed the mast and started rocking the boat from side to side.

Oh, don't do that! she thought.

But just as she'd feared, the boat capsized. The boys tumbled into the chilly billows. From the way they thrashed about it was obvious they couldn't swim!

Ida threw her cleaning cloth into the sink and bolted out the door, startling her mother and father. Her heavy skirt tangled against her legs as she flew over the rocks. As she struggled to drag the boat into the water, all she could think about was reaching the boys in time. Every second counted when people were in danger of drowning.

The roaring wind kept trying to hold her back. And stormy seas picked up her boat then slammed it down into the foamy swells. But Ida fought back with an unrelenting pull on the oars. She had to help the boys before it was too late!

When she reached the wreck, Ida was relieved to find the boys hadn't yet drowned, though that fate seemed to be edging closer with every swell that ducked them under.

"Go get help," one fellow gasped when he saw Ida. "Hurry!"

"*I'll* help you," Ida called back.

"But, but... you're a *girl.*"

Ida was too busy to answer the foolish remark. Her only thought was to pluck them from sea.

As she edged her boat closer, Father's words of caution rang in her ears. *The stern, Ida! Always pull 'em in from the stern or they'll tip you over, too!* It had been Father's strongest advice when she was learning to handle the boat.

The sea was picking up fury, rolling up and down like mountains and valleys in a dizzying way.

While fighting to keep her feet planted firmly on the slick floorboards, Ida swiped a tangle of loose-flying hair from her eyes just in time to see one of the boys lose his grip on the sinking hull.

Her arms shot out to reach him, but he disappeared in the salty foam.

"Hurry, girl! Hurry!" the other boys shouted, struggling to hold on.

Ida knew exactly what she had to do. She peered hard into the water then grasped the limp boy's jacket when he resurfaced. Pulling him closer, she heaved with all her might until he was over the stern at last. He was coughing up plenty of water, but thankfully alive.

One safely in, and three to go.

Ida turned back for the other boys. The sea seemed bent on keeping them in its deadly clutches, tossing them about and ducking them under, away from her arms. But she stubbornly refused to let that happen.

Clenching her jaw, she reached over the stern again and again, tugging and heaving until all the boys were safely aboard.

Ida's arms ached sorely and her lungs felt ready to burst. But she raced the wind to bring her soggy passengers back to the lighthouse.

Cups of soothing hot tea helped revive the frozen teenagers while they dried at the kitchen stove. No longer daring and wild, they meekly revealed their identities. Two fellows were sons of wealthy Newport merchants; the others were visitors from Philadelphia.

The boys shied away from further conversation. Ida sensed their extreme discomfort, secretly wondering which was bothering them most, losing an expensive sailboat or having to be rescued by a *girl.*

"Shall we go?" Ida said softly when all four were dry enough and the sea had calmed.

She rowed them back to Newport's shore, where they disappeared before she'd turned the boat around to head home.

That evening at dinner, Rud, Hosea and Hattie were still full of noisy talk over the daring rescue. But Ida was more interested in helping Father eat his chowder.

Mother shook her head slowly, frowning. "Those foolish boys hardly thanked you," she said to Ida. "Why, you risked life and limb to save them."

Visions of Grace Darling flashed through Ida's mind. "I don't need any thanks for doing what's right," she whispered with conviction. "Those boys would've drowned had I not gone to help them."

After a sideways glance toward Father, she added, "Besides, saving lives is a lighthouse keeper's responsibility."

Mother sighed and reached over to pat Ida's hand gently. "You're a good girl, Idawalley Zoradia Lewis."

As Ida picked up the spoon to feed her father another sip of chowder, she detected a smile twitching at his thin purple lips.

Rud's Lost Skiffs

The years passed quickly. The terrible Civil War had come and gone, Newport was growing by leaps and bounds, and Mary had gotten married. But Ida's life changed little. The house, the beacon and her family still claimed her days and nights.

One February day, close to Ida's twenty-fourth birthday, the temperature dropped so low it set a record around Newport. Ida shivered under her shawl as she scrubbed carrots at the sink and thought of Rud. She hoped he wouldn't freeze to death coming home across the water. He'd taken on all sorts of odd jobs in town to help out with expenses because the four hundred dollars a year the government paid Father as official keeper never seemed to stretch very far.

Now and then Ida threw a tender glance toward her mother. She looked so frail in the old black rocking chair.

Worry and exhaustion pinched her face even as she dozed. Ida knew it was from the seemingly endless nursing. Hosea, too, had come down with the wretched lung sickness that plagued Hattie, and both were suffering through another long bout.

Ida had come to believe the dampness of the lighthouse had caused their illness. Before the thick new floor and walls were poured in the cellar, there'd been water inside the house as well as all around it, having seeped straight up through the rocks.

At that moment, Father shuffled into the room, leaning hard on his cane. He dropped into his favorite chair near the stove and began cleaning his telescope with a soft cloth. The instrument was his only connection to the outside world these days. He'd pass away the hours at the window or open door, scanning the harbor and sharing everything he saw. Ida was so thankful his speech had returned with time. Chatting with him had always been one of her greatest joys.

Now, Ida was just about to ask if he agreed with her idea about dampness and lung sickness when she suddenly heard cries for help.

She dropped the carrots into the sink and dashed outside to scan the misty waters.

A small boat was halfway under the waves!

Without a second thought, Ida pulled her shawl tighter and launched her boat into the numbing blasts of air. She rowed hard and fast over the freezing waters.

As she drew closer to the wreck, her breath caught in her throat. It was Rud's treasured skiff! A man in a soldier's uniform clung to it for dear life. A very *drunk* man from the looks of him.

Rud had saved every spare penny to buy the boat. It was his only means of getting to work. Ida knew he always left the skiff trustingly near Jones's bridge on Newport's shore.

"Save me!" the soldier blubbered again as he bobbed deeper into the swells.

There wasn't time for another second of wondering. Drunk or not, the man needed help, even if he was a thief.

Ida flew into action. The icy water penetrated her long woolen sleeves as she reached over the stern. She could hardly feel her arms as she wrapped them around the soldier and gave a mighty heave.

But the man refused to budge. Instead he dangled drunkenly in the water, like a floating lump of seaweed.

He's heavier than a dead whale! Ida thought.

She drew in a deep breath and gave another fierce tug.

Like a bolt of lightning, searing pain shot up and down her spine. It brought tears to her eyes and undid her grip. The half-drowned soldier was slipping under!

Ida chased the pain from her thoughts and reached into the water again. Bringing the man in was all that mattered. Once she had a tight hold, Ida tugged stubbornly, inch by inch, until the soldier's floppy body came over the stern and into the boat.

The trip back to the lighthouse seemed to take forever. Every stroke of the oars was a painful effort. To make things worse, the icy gusts kept trying to send her in the opposite direction. But with each glance at the pitiful looking soldier sprawled on the floorboards, Ida pulled harder.

She was glad to see Mother waiting on the rocks. Together they dragged the soggy, limp fellow up to the house and into the warm kitchen, where a pot of strong coffee eventually brought him back to his senses.

Wrapped in a thick dry jacket fetched from Rud's bedroom, the soldier shyly confessed he and two companions had stolen the skiff instead of walking the mile-long road back to Fort Adams where they were garrisoned. The sprawling fort, named for President John Adams, lay to the west on the cliff near Brenton's Cove.

"I don't reckon you've seen my buddies?" the soldier asked in a quivering voice.

Ida frowned as she shook her head slowly, hoping the other men had been able enough swimmers to reach shore. She didn't want to think they might have drowned before she arrived at the wreck.

Later, when the soldier was fully recovered, Ida ferried him to the mainland. He walked off into the winter mist without another word, still wearing Rud's warm jacket.

Less than a year later, Ida had nearly finished her lantern room chores when she glanced out the window to find another wintry gale churning the harbor waters into small peaks of white froth.

Suddenly, her eyes widened with disbelief.

"Oh no! Not Rud's *new* skiff!"

The boat was upside-down and sinking. Three men bobbed alongside, doused by the stormy waters.

Though her back still ached plenty, Ida was in her boat in no time. Pulling hard against the wind, she rowed toward the men. She could plainly hear their howls for help as they coughed the salty sea from their mouths.

Then one fellow noticed Ida's approach. "Oh Holy Virgin, have you come down from Heaven to save me?" he cried.

Ida had to bite her lip to keep from laughing at the ridiculous notion.

"I *have* come to save you, though I'm just a lighthouse keeper's daughter."

Once the men were safely in the boat, they explained through chattering teeth they were farmhands employed by the rich Mr. Belmont. They'd only "borrowed" the handy skiff to chase after a prize sheep.

"In the blink of an eye, that wooly wonder dived off the wharf and splashed into the tide," moaned the fellow with the bushy beard.

"Look there!" cried the thinnest of the three. "He's being swept toward the open sea. Oh, can't you save him, too?" he pleaded. "Mr. Belmont will have our heads on a platter for this!"

Ida looked toward the harbor mouth. Sure enough, a ball of whiteness was bobbing in the swells. She felt as if her blood might soon turn to solid ice from the cold, but she loved animals too much to refuse.

Quickly, Ida set the hapless men on shore and rowed back over the waves.

When she reached the drowning sheep, she found the powerful outgoing tide a battle in itself. If she didn't act fast enough both she and the poor animal could wind up in the bottomless Atlantic!

But the more Ida tried getting a rope around the terrified animal, the harder it fought her off, throwing up a storm of waterspouts into the icy wind.

Now Ida was the one tasting the salty sea. "I'm not giving up, fella," she gasped stubbornly. "You might as well let me have my way."

Eventually, Ida's firm resolve proved more powerful than the poor sheep's terror.

When the farmhands glimpsed Ida heading toward shore with their lost charge safely in tow they began howling again, but this time for joy. They jumped up and down as if they were trying to reach the moon.

Ida was soaked to the skin and almost too weary to breathe. Still, she couldn't help laughing hard at the silly sight of them. In fact, she laughed all the way back to the lighthouse, even though poor Rud had lost another skiff to the sea.

The local newspaper published a few scant lines about this latest rescue, though it seemed the townspeople paid the report little mind.

Ida never gave her adventures a second thought either. She'd only been doing her duty, and there was nothing special about that.

The Famous Rescue

Ida awoke one March morning feeling as low and gray as the skies over the harbor. A nasty cold had her feverish and aching.

As the hours passed, snow began to flurry down. Ida was glad Hattie was staying with friends in their snug little house in town. Rud, too, was away from home. He'd found work as a seaman and was off on another short trip. Only Hosea was around, working for hours on a small side table he'd fashioned to add to the parlor's sparse furnishings.

The weather grew worse as the day wore on. In the early twilight brought on by the storm, waves thundered ever harder over the rocks, and every windowpane in the house trembled with each gust of roaring wind.

Ida, still feeling as miserable as the weather, welcomed a brief rest before dinner and settled near the warmth of the stove. Old Matey lazed nearby, along with Queen Victoria, the furry gray kitten Hattie brought home in February as a gift for Ida's twenty-seventh birthday.

As Ida listened to the fury of the storm, she prayed that every ship was anchored safely in port. The unsettling thought prompted another look outside. She stole past her napping father and went to the window.

Except for the mad swirl of snowflakes and rain, hardly anything more was visible. It was as if their little island stood alone in the world. Father's long-ago words rose unbidden from a deep store of memory. *When a fierce storm is blowing with howling winds and battering sea, this pile of rocks can be a rightly godawful place.*

It's true, Ida thought, *every last word.*

After tying a warm towel round her shoulders, she went back to her chair and propped her stocking feet closer to the oven hoping to drive away her chill.

"A dreadful squall, with snow yet!" Ida announced through sniffles when her mother came in from the parlor. "There'll be no closing eyes tonight, for certain."

"Why don't you take a few minutes' nap," Mother said, giving the pot of soup a quick stir. "I'll make sure all's well with the light."

Minutes later, Ida heard her mother's shouts. "Oh my God, Ida! A boat has keeled over!"

Ida leaped from her chair. As she flew out the door, she called for Hosea to follow her.

The towel round Ida's shoulders flapped madly in the howling gusts. Her hair whipped in every direction. Still, Ida could hear a weak cry for help.

Squinting into the pelting snow and icy rain, Ida spied the wreck. She sprinted toward her boat, ignoring the stabs of jagged rocks under her stocking feet. Before Hosea had both his legs aboard, Ida pushed off and rowed into the storm.

Angry waves crested like foamy serpents ready to strike. One after another, they came crashing over the boat, stealing breath and blinding eyes.

Ida fought to keep a steady hand on the oars. "Pray the sea doesn't swallow anyone before we get there," she said, breathing hard.

Hosea clung fiercely to his seat. "Pray we get there at all!" It was no secret that even in good weather, he'd never been fond of the sea.

The boat rose and fell with fury. Breaking swells deepened the icy water round their feet.

"I think we might go under!" Hosea shouted.

"I won't allow it," Ida said defiantly. Her knuckles whitened with strain as she worked the oars. "Just hold tight. We're almost there."

They pulled alongside the bobbing wreck at last. Two half-drowned men clung to the last of the sinking hull, no longer able to cry out.

Before Ida could swing the boat to the right position, Hosea leaned over to grab one of the men. With a frightening swoop the boat tipped to the side, threatening to send them both into the icy sea.

"No, Hosea!" Ida gasped, trying to regain her hold on the oars. "Only from the *stern*. Let *me* bring them in."

The snowy wind and churning sea seemed relentless. But almost daring the elements to topple her, Ida held steady as she extended an oar to one of the men.

At first the terrified man was reluctant to give up his death grip on the hull. But after coaxing shouts, he grabbed on. Ida pulled hard to bring him closer to the stern then lifted him from the water with a mighty tug, right into Hosea's waiting arms.

Wiping snow, rain and salty spray from her eyes, Ida was horrified to discover the second man had slipped from sight!

She brought her drifting boat back to the wreck again and kept plunging her arms into the water until her frozen fingers touched the man's coat. Just as she had him in her grasp another frothy swell swept over them. Robbed of breath a few seconds, Ida stubbornly held on. No way she was going to let the angry sea have him.

The veins in her neck bulged as she summoned every last ounce of strength to wrench the man free.

"You've done it!" Hosea cried as the drowning man flew over the stern in Ida's arms.

A quick smile stretched over Ida's blue lips. "Now all we have to do is get home."

The snowy twilight held no moon or stars. But the Lime Rock Light glowed softly through the storm like a shining path to safety.

Keeping the beam in sight, Ida, exhausted and chilled to the bone, rowed furiously. Her only thought was getting the men to dry clothes and the warmth of the stove. The sagging fellow already appeared too far gone for reviving.

Mother was standing on the rocks when the boat reached shore. She'd been drenched and lashed by the storm, too, anxiously watching and waiting for their return. Now she helped drag the men up to the house.

Ida fetched dry clothes and blankets to go around while Hosea set the men near the stove. Mother quickly prepared hot toddies with the tiniest bit of whiskey kept for such an occasion.

Once the men warmed enough inside and out, they recovered slowly. They introduced themselves as Fort Adams soldiers.

"What fools we were to believe a teenage boy claiming he was an expert sailor," Sergeant James Adams said sadly. "He promised to get us back to the fort safely. Poor fellow disappeared under those terrible waves as soon as the wind toppled the sails."

Private John McLaughlin's eyes filled with grateful tears as he looked at Ida. "I don't know how you did it, girl," he wept. "But I'll be blessing you till the day I die."

Still feeling as cold as harbor ice in January, Ida felt sudden warmth in her cheeks. "I didn't do anything special," she insisted, shaking her head. "I was just doing my job." To escape any further fuss, she jumped up and began pouring another round of toddies and tea.

Before refilling her father's mug, Ida lifted the telescope from his lap and set it on the sill. He'd been watching the whole affair from the window. She could tell from the way he winked at her and gently squeezed her hand that his nerves had finally quieted down.

As always, Ida quickly put the whole affair out of her mind. She had more important things to think about: a lighthouse to keep, a family to care for, and hardly enough hours in a day to see that it all got done.

But as Ida soon discovered, this latest rescue wasn't about to stay forgotten. It seemed word reached the local newspaper. There'd been a longer piece than usual. The lengthy article even included Ida's previous rescues and the hard circumstances of her life.

This time the story jumped from newspaper to newspaper like a frog in a hurry, practically circling the whole *world.*

Swamped With Fame

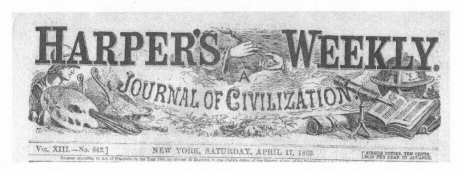

HARPER'S WEEKLY.

A JOURNAL OF CIVILIZATION.

Vol. XIII.—No. 642.]   NEW YORK, SATURDAY, APRIL 17, 1869.   [SINGLE COPIES, TEN CENTS. $4.00 PER YEAR IN ADVANCE.

Ida was astonished when reporters began flooding onto the pale gray rocks a few weeks later. They followed her around as she washed and hung out clothes, asking question after foolish question. They sketched her picture, too, and called her the Heroine of Lime Rock, of all things!

"I just don't know what all this fuss is about," Ida insisted over and over. "Anyone would've done the same."

Unbelievable as it was, the storm of attention grew even more bewildering when a sea of visitors began showing up uninvited.

"I counted six hundred of 'em yesterday alone," Father said early one morning as Ida gently guided him down to the breakfast table. "Never saw anything like it before."

Ida wrinkled her brow into tiny, perplexed waves. "I don't mind when they come to gape at me as if I weren't a regular person just like them," she said with a sigh. "But it's hard to get any work done with hundreds of folks pumping my hand and chasing me around to ask prying kinds of questions all day long. On top of it all I'm told Mr. Boutwell is due to sail over today!"

Generals, admirals, all *sorts* of famous people had already stopped by. Even the handsome new President Ulysses S. Grant had expressed his desire to meet Ida later on in the summer. But only a visit from Mr. George Boutwell could cause the flutters she was feeling in her stomach. He was Secretary of the Treasury, the man in charge of America's lighthouses. Her top boss!

What if he finds fault with something while he's here?

Later, Ida was still straightening up after another round of uninvited visitors when she saw Mr. Boutwell's boat put down anchor. He was first to step onto the rocks, far ahead of the others in his party.

The serious, almost stern, look under his neat dark beard made Ida's heart thump hard, even worse than when the District Inspector came to call. But she took a deep breath, smoothed back her hair, and forced herself to go out and greet him.

When Mr. Boutwell saw Ida, he bowed gallantly before rushing closer. "I wanted to thank you personally for saving the Fort Adams soldiers," he said.

Before Ida could say a word or even nod her head politely, Mr. Boutwell shook her hand, pumping it in a most hearty way. Then he flashed a broad, warm smile.

"And I'd like you to know I'm proud to have a woman in my Department who isn't finicky about getting her hair wet."

Ida forgot all about being nervous. She began laughing so hard her whole body shook. She couldn't help remembering those ladies in Mr. Allen's store that long-ago day. *If only they were here now,* she thought.

"I am happy to meet you, Ida Lewis, as one of the heroic, noble women of the age."

President Ulysses S. Grant

Ida Lewis Day

The city of Newport had proclaimed the upcoming Fourth of July to be "Ida Lewis Day." As the star of the annual parade Ida was to be carried about in a fancy new boat, a gift from the townspeople. A formal presentation of the boat would take place at a ceremony at the end of the parade.

When Ida heard these plans she cringed. "A public demonstration? Never!" she said, as firm as she'd ever been in her life, "There's not money enough in Newport to pay me for riding round the streets for a show."

She had a slight change of heart when she realized the people of Newport might consider her ungrateful. That's when she decided it was her *duty* to oblige their thoughtful intentions.

Ida agreed to appear at the celebration. But at the presentation ceremony *only*. And on *her* terms: No speech! "I never made a speech in my life, and I don't expect to begin now."

Ida's precise conditions were accepted. Colonel Thomas Wentworth Higginson, a famous author living in Newport, offered to be Ida's "voice" at the ceremony.

The day Ida had been dreading broke hot and sunny. At the end of the parade, thousands of the spectators gathered in the little park in front of the old State House for the presentation ceremony.

When Ida arrived, she looked warily at the milling throngs. She'd never seen so many people in one place. Suddenly, the rumble of voices grew louder. She'd been spotted! Then a path in the sea of people opened up like a fast receding tide.

Ida held her breath as she was escorted through. Her stomach felt like a cage full of butterflies, but she walked straight as a ship's mast, thankful to have Mother and Hattie at her side. If only the rest of the family could have been there, too. But Hosea had to watch over Father and the lighthouse. And Rud was off to sea on another short voyage.

"I pray this is over quickly," Ida whispered to Hattie. She hid her face behind a fashionable black lace veil. Hattie had insisted it added a nice touch to the rust-colored silk dress trimmed with black lace. The orange kid gloves were Hattie's idea, too.

"I've never been so fancy-dressed in my entire life," Ida had declared earlier, feeling more discomfort with each new piece of clothing she'd donned. The only thing she took joy in wearing was the beautiful beaded choker circling her neck. It was another one of Mother's treasures from Grandmother Willey.

The gleaming new boat had been set on a platform built for the occasion. Ida could see the name *Rescue* painted on the side. After stepping gingerly inside, her glance darted from the rich mahogany wood to the gold-filled oarlocks and red velvet cushions. She found it nearly impossible to imagine rowing about the harbor in the middle of such elegance.

A sudden hush fell over the crowd as Colonel Higginson and Mr. Francis Brinley appeared at Ida's side, each greeting her with a polite nod and broad smile.

Mr. Brinley was a prominent lawyer and classical scholar. He cleared his throat in a dramatic way then sailed swiftly through his flowery presentation speech with an orator's voice, recounting Ida's courage in the face of danger and praising her service to humanity. At the end he turned to Ida and said the boat came to her with the kindest wishes of the inhabitants of Newport.

As the air thundered with cheers, Ida felt her cheeks growing hotter than the July sun overhead. But she kept her dignified position and faced the crowd staunchly, praying this ordeal wouldn't take much longer.

Then Colonel Higginson took a step forward. He held up his hands as he smiled at the crowd. "I am requested by Miss Lewis to return thanks in her name to the donors, and to the citizens of Newport," he began. "She is grateful to you for your acknowledgment of what seemed to her a simple act of duty."

Colonel Higginson's words had barely ended when rising voices began to chant: "Show us your face! We want to see the face of Ida Lewis!"

Ida flinched at the sudden, new demands. But she was afraid it might appear as disrespect if she were to refuse. Taking a deep breath she rose to her feet and slowly lifted her veil.

More cheers exploded from the satisfied throng, much louder than before. Ida didn't know what else to do except snatch the lace handkerchief tucked at her waist and wave it briefly as a hurried kind of thank-you.

At last the ceremony came to an end. A large swarm of the well-wishers trailed behind Ida, Mother and Hattie as they made their way down to the dock where the old lighthouse boat waited. It had been planned that Ida would return later in the day to bring the *Rescue* back to the lighthouse.

Moving as fast as it was possible in a fancy silk dress Ida settled her mother and sister in the boat. Then she removed the silly veil and began pulling hard on the oars. Her only thought was to get home to her beloved, quiet Lime Rock Light.

All of a sudden a man's loud voice boomed from the midst of the wildly waving crowd: "Three cheers for Ida Lewis. She's our Grace Darling of America!"

That made Ida smile. It was her first smile of the day.

Afterword

The famous March rescue of 1869 was by no means the last of Ida's courageous acts.

On a wintry February evening in 1881, cries for help reached her ears once again.

Outside, two Fort Adams soldiers were thrashing about in a dark circle of water, close to drowning! It seemed they'd fallen through the ice while trying to cross the frozen harbor on foot.

Without a second thought Ida grabbed a length of rope and rushed across the frozen harbor toward the drowning men.

The ice was so thin she could hear it crackling under her feet, threatening to drop her, too, into the freezing black waters.

But Ida paid it no mind. She tossed the rope to the men then tugged and heaved with all her determined might until she'd successfully hauled the first man from the black watery hole. Rud, home for a time, helped her drag the other man to safety.

Soon after, Ida was awarded the Gold Lifesaving Medal of the U. S. Lifesaving Service. It was the first time a woman had received this special honor.

Ida often tucked away her many medals and awards in her sewing basket, forever feeling she didn't deserve such things. She was only doing her job!

She once told a reporter, "If there were some people out there who needed help, I would get into my boat and go to them even if I knew I couldn't get back. Wouldn't you?"

The reporter had no reply.

An official count credits Ida with saving about eighteen people over the years, though it's widely believed there were other rescues that never came to light.

Ida herself had no idea how many people she'd saved. It never entered her mind to keep count! Most times she didn't even know the names of those she'd given back their lives.

Ida hadn't been named the *official* keeper of the Lime Rock Light until 1879. The much-deserved appointment came about only after Rhode Island Senator Ambrose Burnside, a Civil War general, helped fight for the recognition due the Heroine of Lime Rock.

Ida tended the Lime Rock Light and watched over the harbor for more than fifty years. It's been said she left only once, during a brief, unsuccessful marriage to Captain William Wilson, a seaman. Then she'd hurried back to the place where her heart truly lay.

Captain Hosea Lewis, Ida's beloved father, died three years after the famous 1869 rescue. In 1883, Hattie and Hosea, Jr. were both claimed by the dreaded consumption (now called tuberculosis) while still in their early thirties.

Then four years later, Ida's mother, also named Idawalley Zoradia, had passed on, too, leaving Ida all alone on the outcropping of rocks in the harbor.

But after a time, Rud gave up his former work and returned to the lighthouse to live with his sister.

Ida's amazing courage and clear thinking never dwindled with age. Her last known rescue took place when she was sixty-four years old. A friend from town had been rowing over for a visit with Ida when she fell overboard.

Some people claimed the woman stood up in the boat to smooth out her dress. But it didn't matter to Ida *why* her friend had splashed into the sea. She knew the woman couldn't swim!

As always, Ida rowed swiftly to the rescue. Afterwards, she prepared a nice hot cup of tea to warm the poor woman as she dried near the lighthouse stove. And more than likely, the two friends even shared a few chuckles about the whole affair.

Then one October day in 1911 Rud found Ida unconscious on the floor. She'd suffered a stroke, just as her father had. And strangely enough, it happened at the same time of year!

Some friends thought Ida's illness was brought on by extreme worry. Supposedly there'd been "scoldings" from her superiors because she'd filled out new, modern forms incorrectly.

Besides that, a report had appeared in the *Newport Daily News* hinting that the Lime Rock Light might be abolished. For Ida, this would have been unthinkable.

No one knows for sure what really happened, though it was true Ida had never wanted to live anywhere but at her beloved lighthouse.

Ida's own words expressed her innermost feelings many times in the past:

"This is home to me and I hope the good Lord will take me away when I have to leave it."

On October 24, three days after her stroke, Ida Lewis took her last breath. When the word went out, all the ships in the harbor tolled their bells, like a symphony of sad news.

At the end of church services on funeral day, Ida was buried in Newport's Common Ground Cemetery on Farewell Street.

A fitting gravestone was erected after Mary Dewick, the sixteen-year-old daughter of one of Ida's friends, went door-to-door to collect money.

Almost certainly, Ida would have been pleased by the carved granite marker bought with the donations. Part of the inscription reads:

The Grace Darling of America
Keeper of Lime Rock Lighthouse
Newport Harbor

The little house Ida left on that long-ago June day still stands at 283 Spring Street, though her beloved Lime Rock Light is now the Ida Lewis Yacht Club, a private organization.

Fortunately, some of Ida's surviving memorabilia is in the protective hands of the Newport Historical Society.

American lighthouses fell under the jurisdiction of the U.S. Coast Guard in 1939. Several years ago, the service honored Ida's memory by naming a new cutter the *USCGC IDA LEWIS.*

One of the ship's most important duties is search and rescue, just like the Heroine of Lime Rock.

Recently, the cutter's crew discovered Ida's grave had been terribly neglected through the years. With no one left to care for it, the cemetery plot was shabby and overgrown, sadly unfitting for a famous heroine.

That would never do! The Coasties went to work at once. They weeded, polished and generally cleaned things up. After that they put up four gleaming, granite lighthouses at the corners, attached by steel chains.

Now, the ordinary girl who performed extraordinary deeds has a suitable, everlasting place of honor.

"I never thought of danger when people needed me. At such times you're busy thinking of other things."

Yours truly

Ida Lewis

February 24th 1867

16734656R00050

Made in the USA
Middletown, DE
21 December 2014